Tales from the Shadows

Tales from the Shadows

Paul Zartman

CONTENTS

The Long Drive

Jake had always loved road trips. The open road, the wind in his hair, the hum of his old 1998 Toyota Camry—driving was his escape. So when he got a text from his buddy, Tom, asking for a favor to pick him up from a town called Hallow Oaks, Jake didn't think twice.

It was supposed to be a simple drive—two hours down an old highway that cut through miles of empty countryside. But halfway through, his GPS lost signal. The sun had set, and the night consumed the road in darkness. There were no other cars, no streetlights, just the infinite stretch of asphalt ahead.

Jake flipped on the radio to break the eerie silence, but all he got was static. Then, the headlights flickered.

He thought it was just a glitch, but the hairs on his neck stood up. Something didn't feel right. The road seemed to stretch forever, like he was driving in circles. He hadn't seen a single turnoff, sign, or landmark in over an hour. Was he even going the right way?

His phone buzzed—a text from Tom: "Where are you?"

Jake rechecked his map. Still no signal. But then, something caught his eye in the rearview mirror. A shadow darting just beyond the reach of his taillights. He quickly glanced back, but the road behind him was empty.

Jake's grip on the steering wheel tightened as unease crept over him. He was not alone on this road.

Jake's pulse quickened as he continued driving. He glanced again at the mirror, hoping to catch another glimpse of the shadow. Nothing. The road stretched on, seemingly endless.

Another message from Tom popped up: "You're late. Hurry up."

The headlights flickered again, and Jake cursed under his breath. He was sure now something was wrong with the car. In the distance, a figure appeared ahead, standing by the side of the road, holding a thumb out—a hitchhiker.

Jake slowed the car. The man wore a tattered jacket and had his face hidden beneath a hood. Jake usually didn't pick up strangers, especially not at night, but something told him this guy might know where he was.

As the car stopped, the man leaned down, his face still obscured in shadow. "Where you headed?" the hitchhiker asked, his voice husky.

"Uh, Hallow Oaks," Jake replied hesitantly.

The hitchhiker stood still for a moment before opening the passenger door. "I know the way," he said. "But it's not a place you want to go."

Jake felt a cold shiver run down his spine. Against his better judgment, he let the man in. The hitchhiker said nothing as they drove, only staring out the window. The silence was suffocating.

Suddenly, the man spoke. "You'll see things on this road. Things you shouldn't follow."

"What do you mean?" Jake asked, glancing at him. But the hitchhiker didn't respond. His eyes were fixed on something ahead. Jake followed his gaze and saw a glowing figure standing in the middle of the road.

Jake slammed on the brakes, his heart pounding in his chest. The glowing figure seemed to hover just ahead of the car, its form flickering like a ghost caught between worlds. It was hard to make out any details—it was as if the figure wasn't solid, like a shimmer of light that refused to stay still.

"Do you see that?" Jake asked, turning to the hitchhiker. But the man wasn't in his seat.

The passenger door was wide open, and the hitchhiker was gone. Jake's mind raced. How could he have left without him noticing? He hadn't even heard the door open. Panic clawed at him, but he forced himself to stay calm.

The figure on the road moved slowly toward the car. Jake could now make out more of its shape—a woman, her face pale and lifeless, eyes black voids. She raised her hand and pointed directly at him.

Jake's foot pressed on the gas pedal instinctively. The car lurched forward, passing through the figure as if it wasn't there. His hands were shaking, his heart pounding in his ears. He had no idea what he had just seen, but he knew one thing—he needed to get off this road.

But as he drove, the landscape around him started to change. The trees seemed to twist and contort, their branches reaching out like skeletal hands. The road, once familiar, now felt like a tunnel leading deeper into darkness.

There was no turning back now.

Jake's knuckles turned white as he gripped the steering wheel. His breath came in shallow bursts as the weight of isolation pressed down on him. Every fiber of his being screamed that he should turn around, but the road no longer offered that choice. The strange woman—was she real? A hallucination? He couldn't make sense of it.

He reached for the radio again, desperate for any connection to normalcy. As his fingers brushed the dial, static filled the speakers once more. But through the crackling interference, Jake heard something—faint whispers.

His heart pounded harder. He turned the volume up, trying to make out the voices. It sounded like...laughter. Distorted, distant, but unmistakably human. Then, amidst the eerie din, a voice cut through the static, clear as day.

"Don't stop."

Jake recoiled, his hand jerking away from the radio. The voice sounded too close, as if someone were sitting beside him. He rechecked the passenger seat, and it was empty. His skin crawled with the sensation of being watched.

He floored the gas pedal, eyes scanning the road ahead. The last thing he wanted was to encounter another phantom. But the voice, the laughter—it didn't stop. It grew louder, filling the car and surrounding him like a fog.

Then the headlights flickered again. This time, they ultimately died.

The darkness was absolute. Without the headlights, Jake couldn't see a thing. His foot slammed the brake, and the car skidded to a halt, its tires screeching against the asphalt. The engine sputtered and died, leaving him alone in the black void.

He fumbled for his phone, hoping to use its flashlight, but the screen stayed dark when he pressed the power button. There was no signal, no power, nothing. He was trapped.

Jake sat in the car, his breath shallow, trying to gather his thoughts. He couldn't stay here; that much was clear. But stepping outside into the unknown terrified him. He could feel something lurking in the darkness.

A soft tap came from outside his window.

Jake froze. Another tap—this time louder. He slowly turned his head toward the sound. His window was fogged, but he could make out the faint outline of a hand pressed against the glass.

His heart pounded in his chest as the tapping grew more insistent. Suddenly, it stopped, replaced by a low, guttural whisper.

"Get out."

Jake's pulse quickened, and panic rose in his throat. He couldn't stay in the car, but the thought of stepping into the darkness outside was equally horrifying. His mind raced, and he tried to think of a way out. Maybe the tapping was just his imagination—perhaps he was losing his mind.

But then the door handle jiggled.

The whisper returned, more insistent now. "Get out."

Jake's breath hitched. He had no choice. With trembling hands, he unlocked the door and slowly pushed it open. Cold air rushed in, carrying the thick scent of damp earth and decay. The world outside was shrouded in an impenetrable fog, swallowing everything beyond a few feet.

He stepped out, keeping close to the car as his eyes darted around. The fog seemed to shift and move like a living thing, hiding whatever was out there. He could hear faint footsteps in the distance, echoing through the mist.

Then, without warning, a figure emerged from the fog—a tall and gaunt man wearing the same tattered jacket as the hitchhiker.

"You shouldn't have stopped," the man said, his voice low and distorted.

Jake backed away, his heart pounding. The man's face was twisted, unnatural, as if it didn't belong to him. He stepped closer, his eyes black voids like the woman on the road.

Jake turned and ran.

Jake's feet pounded against the asphalt as he sprinted down the road. The fog was disorienting, swallowing up the sound of his footsteps, making it impossible to tell how far he had run. His lungs burned, his muscles ached, but he didn't dare stop.

Behind him, the sound of footsteps grew closer. They weren't running—they were strolling, deliberately, sending chills down his spine. He glanced back but saw nothing, just the swirling fog.

Suddenly, the road beneath his feet disappeared.

Jake stumbled, falling hard onto a soft, wet surface. He looked down, realizing he was no longer on the road but in the woods. Twisted, gnarled trees surrounded him, their branches forming a canopy blocking the sky. The ground beneath him was soft, almost like a swamp, and the air was thick with the scent of rot and decay.

Jake scrambled to his feet, panic surging through him. He had no idea how he'd ended up here. The road was gone, swallowed by the fog and the strange forest. His ragged breathing and the faint leaves rustling in the distance were the only sound.

He turned in circles, trying to get his bearings, but the forest seemed to close in on him, the trees pressing closer, their branches reaching down like claws. His mind raced—had he blacked out? Was this some nightmare?

The footsteps returned, louder now, echoing through the trees.

Jake spun around. In the distance, barely visible through the mist, was the shadowy figure of the man in the tattered jacket. His outline flickered like a mirage, but his presence was unmistakable.

The figure stood still, watching.

Jake's heart pounded as the man began to speak again, his voice carrying unnaturally through the forest. "There's no escaping this place. The road calls to those it chooses. You've been chosen."

Jake stumbled backward, his mind reeling. "What are you talking about?" he shouted, his voice hoarse. "What is this place?"

The man's form flickered again, and this time, his face appeared more evident—hollow, pale, with deep black voids where his eyes should have been. "It's the road. It wants you."

Suddenly, the ground beneath Jake's feet shifted, pulling him down. He fell, his hands sinking into the wet earth as if the forest was trying to consume him. He screamed, struggling to free himself, but the more he fought, the deeper he sank.

The earth swallowed Jake's legs, pulling him deeper into the cold, clammy soil. He gasped for air, his chest tightening as the ground came alive. Tendrils of mud and roots wrapped around his arms, dragging him down.

"Help!" he screamed, his voice ragged and desperate, but the forest was silent except for the relentless whispers in the fog.

Just as his head was about to be submerged, something cold and hard gripped his wrist. A hand—bony and freezing—yanked him free of the sinking ground, pulling him up with unnatural strength. Jake gasped for breath and again found himself face-to-face with the hitchhiker.

But the man's features were even more distorted now. His skin was cracked, like ancient wood, and his eyes were sunken, black pits. "You don't belong here," he rasped, yanking Jake to his feet. "The road oesn't let you leave, but you can still outrun it. For now.—forore Jake could speak, the hitchhiker pushed him forward. "Run!" the man shouted, his voice echoing eerily through the trees.

Jake didn't need to be told twice. He ran, his legs trembling but fueled by pure terror. The forest twisted and warped around him, the trees bending impossibly, their gnarled branches reaching out to grab him. The hitchhiker was gone every time he glanced back, but the whispering voices remained, calling his name and beckoning him deeper into the woods.

Just when he thought his lungs would burst, Jake stumbled out of the trees and onto solid asphalt. The road. He was back.

But it wasn't the same. The air felt wrong—thicker and oppressive. The darkness was impenetrable, swallowing the world around him. There were no stars or moon, just an endless void. The road stretched out before him like a black ribbon into nothingness.

Then, in the distance, he saw a single, flickering light. Headlights.

Relief surged through Jake's body as he staggered toward the distant headlights. He waved his arms, hoping to flag down the car, but a sinking feeling settled in his gut as he got closer.

The car wasn't moving.

It sat idly in the middle of the road, its headlights flickering as if it had been abandoned. Jake slowed down, his breath catching in his throat. Something about the car felt familiar.

He approached cautiously, his footsteps echoing unnaturally loud in the silence. The car was old, with chipped and rusted paint. Then Jake froze. His heart stopped as he saw the license plate.

It was his car.

The realization hit him like a punch to the gut. The car he had been driving—the one he had left behind in the fog—was sitting right in front of him, untouched, its engine still running, the door slightly ajar.

Jake's mind raced. How was this possible? He had left it behind miles ago. He had run for hours—hadn't he?

Slowly, he approached the driver's side door. His fingers trembled as he reached for the handle. A figure slumped in the driver's seat as the door creaked open. Jake stepped back, his breath catching in his throat.

It was him.

Jake stared at his own lifeless body, slumped over the wheel, eyes wide open, staring blankly ahead. His mind reeled, unable to process what he was seeing. This had to be a nightmare, a trick of the fog.

The headlights flickered, and suddenly, the lifeless version of himself twitched. The head slowly turned, its vacant eyes locking onto him.

"You can't run," the figure whispered, its voice a guttural rasp. "You're already part of the road."

Jake stumbled backward, his heart racing as his doppelgänger's twisted face leered at him from the driver's seat. The figure's voice grew louder, the words slithering through the air like a curse. "It won't let you leave."

Panicking, Jake turned and ran down the road, but every step felt heavier than the last. The asphalt beneath his feet seemed to stretch endlessly, each mile longer than the one before, as if the road was pulling him deeper into its grasp. The whispers in the fog grew louder, surrounding him, echoing his fears.

"You're one of us now."

Jake ran harder, his legs burning, but the road never ended, no matter how far he went. The forest loomed on either side, watching him, waiting. The flickering headlights of his car remained visible behind him no matter how far he ran.

Then, in the distance, Jake saw the exact glowing figure that had appeared on the road earlier: the woman with the black eyes. She stood in the middle of the road, waiting for him, her form shifting and flickering like a mirage.

Exhausted and terrified, Jake slowed to a stop. He was trapped. There was no escaping the road, no escaping what it wanted from him.

The woman raised her hand again, pointing directly at him. "It's time," she whispered.

The ground beneath Jake's feet began to tremble. Cracks appeared in the asphalt, glowing faintly with an otherworldly light. The whispers grew louder, more insistent, as the road seemed to come alive, ready to consume him.

Jake fell to his knees, the weight of the road pressing down on him, pulling him into the darkness. His vision blurred, and the last thing he saw was the woman's face, her black eyes staring into his soul.

The road had claimed him.

And somewhere, deep in the fog, the hitchhiker waited for the next traveler to pass by, ready to guide them into the endless nightmare that was The Long Drive.

2

The Collector's Curse

Todd Bishop was a man of expensive tastes. A collector of rare artifacts, antiquities, and curiosities, he prided himself on owning pieces that no one else could. His vast collection filled his mansion, from ancient Egyptian relics to voodoo dolls from the Caribbean.

But he wanted one item more than anything—the mysterious artifact known only as "The Veil of Shadows." Said to be cursed, it was rumored to grant its owner unimaginable power, but at a terrible price. Few believed in the stories, but Todd didn't care. He wanted it for the prestige, the thrill of owning something so dangerous.

One evening, as Todd sipped his vintage wine, a letter arrived. There was no return address, just an old wax seal with a strange symbol. Curious, he opened it.

"I know what you seek. Meet me at the Old Mill. Midnight. Bring no one."

Todd chuckled. It sounded like a scene from a cheap horror movie. But his desire for the Veil of Shadows outweighed any fear. He'd only play along to see what this mysterious person had to offer.

At midnight, Todd arrived at the decrepit Old Mill. Inside, in the flickering candlelight, a figure waited. Cloaked and hooded, the figure's face was hidden in shadow.

"I hear you're a man who likes to collect the extraordinary," the figure rasped. "I have something for you... but it comes with a warning."

Todd smirked. "I've heard warnings before. Show me."

A small box, ancient and carved from a strange, black stone, emerged from the figure's cloak. A dark, tattered veil was revealed inside when the figure opened it.

"The Veil of Shadows," the figure whispered. "Its power is real. But once you possess it, it will possess you."

Todd barely heard the warning. His eyes were locked on the veil, his desire burning brighter. "Name your price."

The figure chuckled softly. "There's no price. It's a gift. But remember, once it's yours, there's no going back."

Todd, blinded by greed, took the box without hesitation.

Back home, Todd placed the Veil of Shadows in his collection room. It sat on a pedestal, illuminated by soft lighting, casting an eerie shadow on the walls.

He admired it from every angle, the strange fabric seeming to shift and shimmer in the dim light. It was like nothing he'd ever seen before. An odd feeling washed over him as he gazed at it—a mixture of triumph and unease.

That night, Todd couldn't sleep. He tossed and turned, visions of the veil haunting his dreams. Shadows danced on his bedroom walls, shapes moving just out of sight. He could hear soft and indistinct whispers as if they were inside his head.

By morning, Todd was exhausted. His eyes were bloodshot, his nerves frayed. But he brushed it off. "Just a rough night," he muttered to himself. "It's nothing."

But the whispers didn't stop.

Over the next few days, Todd noticed strange things around the mansion. Items in his collection would be moved, not by his hand. Mirrors seemed to show reflections that weren't his own, and when he walked by, he could swear he saw figures moving in the corners of his vision.

The Veil of Shadows became an obsession. He found himself drawn to it, staring at it for hours. The whispers grew louder, more insistent.

They were calling him, beckoning him closer to the veil, promising him something... but what?

At night, the shadows in his room grew darker and more profound. They seemed to pulse and shift, crawling along the walls and floor and inching closer to his bed. The air grew thick and suffocating as if something was watching him, waiting.

Todd tried to ignore it and convince himself it was just his mind playing tricks. But the longer he denied it, the worse it became.

One night, as he lay in bed, unable to sleep, the whispers became words.

"Wear the veil. Become one with the shadows."

Todd sat up, heart pounding. The voice was no longer inside his head. It was in the room with him.

Todd stared at the Veil of Shadows from across the room, its dark fabric seeming to ripple like water. The voice continued, soft but commanding.

"Wear it."

Against his better judgment, Todd rose from the bed. His body moved as if in a trance, each step bringing him closer to the pedestal. He reached out, fingers trembling, and lifted the veil from its resting place.

The moment it touched his skin, an overwhelming coldness spread. The veil clung to him, wrapping around his head like a living thing. His vision darkened, and the room seemed to dissolve into shadow.

For a moment, Todd felt a rush of power. The whispers were no longer distant but clear, speaking of control, dominance, and immortality. He felt invincible and untouchable.

But then the darkness turned on him.

Suddenly, the shadows began to tighten around his throat, squeezing, suffocating him. His heartbeat thundered in his ears as the veil constricted, pulling him deeper into the void. He tried to rip it off, but his hands passed right through it as if it had become a part of him.

The shadows whispered again, but this time, they were laughing.

When Todd finally tore the veil from his head, he stumbled backward, gasping for air. He looked around, disoriented. The room was the same, but something was wrong—very wrong.

His reflection in the mirror was not his own.

Todd stared at the glass, horrified. The figure looking back at him was gaunt and pale, with hollow eyes and a twisted smile. It mimicked his every move, but it wasn't him. It was something else, something darker.

He smashed the mirror in a panic, but the reflection remained, now shattered into a dozen grinning faces. The whispers in his head were no longer faint—they were deafening.

"You belong to us now. The shadows never let go."

As the days passed, Todd felt desperate. He tried to rid himself of the veil by throwing it into the fire, locking it in a vault, and burying it in the garden. But no matter what he did, the veil always returned, sitting on its pedestal as if it had never left.

He consulted experts, priests, and anyone who might have a solution. But they recoiled in fear every time he mentioned the Veil of Shadows.

"The veil is cursed," one old man had said. "Once it chooses you, there's no escaping it."

The whispers continued to torment Todd. The shadows in his home grew bolder, moving of their own accord, twisting into monstrous shapes that clawed at his mind. Every night, they came closer, suffocating him with their cold, dark tendrils.

Todd could feel himself slipping away.

One evening, Todd received a surprise visitor—the exact cloaked figure who had given him the veil. "You seem... troubled," the figure said, the faintest hint of mockery in their voice.

"Take it back," Todd begged. "I'll pay anything. I don't want it anymore."

The figure chuckled darkly. "There's no price, Todd. The veil will remain yours until it takes what it's owed."

Todd's blood ran cold. "What does it want?"

"Your soul, of course," the figure said. "That's the power price. Surely, you knew that?"

Todd's dreams grew darker each night, and the shadows more relentless. His body weakened as if the shadows were draining his very life. No matter how hard he fought, he couldn't escape them.

The whispers became unbearable. They spoke of darkness eternal, of a fate worse than death. Todd knew his time was running out.

One night, as the shadows closed in, he made a decision. He would destroy the veil, even if it killed him.

Todd gathered all his strength and stormed into his collection room. The veil sat on the pedestal, waiting for him, almost mocking in its stillness.

He picked it up with trembling hands and ran to the basement, where he had set up a hotter furnace than anything he'd used. He threw the veil into the flames, watching as it was engulfed by fire.

For a moment, Todd felt relief.

But then the shadows descended.

Todd screamed as the shadows tore through him, pulling him apart piece by piece. The veil was not destroyed—it had simply returned to where it belonged. The whispers laughed as his soul was consumed by darkness, his body crumbling into ash.

When the shadows cleared, there was nothing left of Todd Bishop.

The mansion sat in silence, the Veil of Shadows again resting on its pedestal, waiting for the next fool to claim it.

3

The Blackwood Legacy

The envelope was heavy, its edges frayed and worn. It arrived on a Tuesday, addressed to Sarah in an elegant and unsettling handwriting. Inside, there was a single handwritten card. The words were few, but they sent a shiver down Sarah's spine:

"You are invited to a gathering of old friends. It is a night of remembrance, a celebration of the past. Come, if you dare."

The card was unsigned, but Sarah knew who it was from. It was an invitation from the Blackwood family, a family she had known since childhood. The Blackwood house, a sprawling Victorian mansion, had always been a place of mystery and intrigue.

Sarah hesitated. She had not seen the Blackwoods in years, and the memories associated with them were bittersweet. But something about the invitation—its wording, its sense of urgency—drew her in. She decided to accept.

Sarah arrived at the Blackwood house the night of the gathering, her heart pounding. The mansion was shrouded in darkness, save for a single light in the attic window. She heard a faint, eerie melody as she approached the front door.

She hesitated for a moment, then took a deep breath and knocked. The door creaked open, revealing a dark, empty hallway. A chill ran down her spine as she stepped inside.

As Sarah stepped into the Blackwood house, she was struck by the oppressive silence. The once-vibrant mansion felt cold and lifeless. The only sound was the faint echo of her footsteps and the eerie melody that seemed to follow her.

She made her way through the darkened hallways, her heart pounding. The air was thick with the scent of decay and something sinister. She tried to shake off the feeling, but it was impossible.

Finally, she reached the attic. The door was slightly ajar, and a sliver of light escaped from the room. She pushed the door open and stepped inside.

The attic was a cavernous space filled with cobwebs and dust. In the center of the room, a long oak table was set with candles and a single, withered bouquet. Surrounding the table were chairs, each occupied by a figure shrouded in shadow.

As Sarah entered the room, the figures turned to face her. She recognized them immediately. They were her old friends, the Blackwood family, but they looked different. Their faces were pale and gaunt, their eyes hollow and devoid of life.

"Welcome, Sarah," a voice said from the head of the table. It was the voice of the family patriarch, Mr. Blackwood. He stood up and approached her, his eyes fixed on her strangely.

"We have been waiting for you," he said. "You are the final piece of the puzzle."

Sarah felt a wave of fear wash over her. She tried to back away, but it was too late. The figures around the table rose from their chairs and began to close in on her.

"It's time," Mr. Blackwood said, his voice chilling. "It's time for the sacrifice."

As the figures closed in on Sarah, she felt a cold dread. She tried to scream, but no sound came out. The room seemed to spin around her as she struggled to break free.

Then, a strange sensation came over her. She felt a warmth spreading through her body, a sense of peace that was utterly at odds with the terror she was experiencing. The figures around her seemed to fade away, replaced by a vision of the past.

She saw herself as a young girl, playing in the Blackwood gardens with Mr. Blackwood's children. She remembered the laughter, the joy, the sense of belonging. But then, something changed. The children disappeared, and Mr. Blackwood's eyes took on a sinister glint.

She saw him performing a dark ceremony to bring back his lost family. But the ritual had gone wrong, and now, years later, he was trying to complete it.

The vision faded, and Sarah found herself standing alone in the attic. The figures were gone, and the room was bathed in a soft, ethereal light. She knew what she had to do.

She approached the table and took the withered bouquet. She placed it on the floor with a heavy heart and lit a candle. Then, she spoke the words she had heard in the vision.

As she spoke, the room began to tremble. The walls seemed to close on her, and a blinding light filled the attic. When the light faded, Sarah stood in a clearing, the Blackwood house nowhere to be seen.

She had escaped, but at a terrible cost. The Blackwood family was gone, their souls forever trapped in the darkness. And Sarah, forever changed by the experience, knew she would never be the same.

4

The Whispering Shadows

The old mansion had loomed over the town of Draymore for as long as anyone could remember. Once grand and imposing, it had decayed into a shadow of its former glory. The locals whispered about strange occurrences—disappearances, lights flickering in the dead of night, and eerie whispers that carried on the wind. No one dared to venture near the place after dark, not even for a dare. Yet, there was a particular lure to it.

Tommy, Allison, Mark, and Jessica—college friends looking for a thrill—decided to test the rumors. What better way to celebrate Halloween than by exploring Draymore's most notorious haunted site?

"Are you guys sure about this?" Jessica asked, her nerves already frayed as the group stood before the mansion's iron gates.

Tommy grinned, flipping a flashlight in his hand. "It's just a spooky old house. What's the worst that could happen?"

They pushed the gates open with a loud creak and approached the entrance. As the door groaned open, a gust of cold air rushed out to greet them. They laughed it off, unaware of the shadows already watching from the darkness within.

The house greeted them with an ominous silence. Dust coated every surface, and cobwebs hung like curtains. The flicker of their flashlights was the only light cutting through the gloom. The faint odor of decay hung in the air.

"Creepy, but not that bad," Mark said, trying to keep his voice steady.

As they ventured deeper, strange things began to happen. A portrait on the wall seemed to watch them, its eyes following their movements. Shadows twisted in the corners, even when no one was moving. Allison laughed nervously, but the others were growing uneasy.

Then, there was a loud thump from upstairs.

"What the hell was that?" Tommy asked, pointing his flashlight toward the staircase.

"Just the house settling," Mark said, though his voice betrayed doubt.

But the sound of slow, deliberate footsteps from the floor above told a different story.

Determined to prove there was nothing to fear, Tommy led them upstairs. The second floor was even darker, and the air seemed heavier and oppressive.

They found an old, dust-covered chest in the attic. Inside was a journal, its leather cover cracked and faded with age. It belonged to Jonathan Crowley, the house's last owner.

Flipping through the pages, they discovered unsettling entries. Crowley had been obsessed with the occult. He wrote of rituals, sacrifices, and an ancient curse that clung to the house like a sickness. He claimed the spirits of those who died within its walls were trapped, unable to move on.

The last entry was scrawled in shaky handwriting: "They whisper to me at night. They wait in the shadows. They want my soul, and I fear I will soon join them."

That night, they decided to stay in the house to finish exploring in the morning. But as darkness fell, the whispers began. At first, they were soft, like the rustling of leaves. But then they grew louder and more precise—voices murmuring unintelligibly.

Jessica was the first to hear them. She sat bolt upright in her sleeping bag, her heart racing. The whispers seemed to come from all around her, circling like predators. She shook Tommy awake, but when he listened, all was silent.

"Just a dream," he muttered, rolling over. But Jessica knew better. She could see shadows moving where there shouldn't be any.

By morning, things had escalated. Mark had gone missing. His bedroll lay undisturbed, but there was no sign of him anywhere in the house. Panic set in as they searched every room, calling his name to no avail.

In the attic, they found footprints from the window to where Mark had been sitting. The journal lay open, with new writing scrawled across the page in Mark's handwriting: "They are inside me. The shadows, they whisper promises."

Allison screamed, backing away from the journal. "We need to leave. Now."

But as they rushed to the front door, it slammed shut with a force that echoed through the manor. The air grew cold, and the shadows deepened, becoming almost solid. Something was keeping them there.

The day dragged on, but the sun never seemed to rise fully. The manor seemed to trap them in a perpetual twilight. Allison grew pale and jittery, muttering to herself. She swore she could see faces in the walls, eyes staring from the darkness.

Tommy tried to stay calm, but the pressure was mounting. He couldn't shake the feeling that they were being watched by something ancient and evil.

On the other hand, Jessica was growing more convinced they had awoken something terrible. As she stared into the mirror, she thought she saw her reflection smile back at her—a twisted, hungry grin that did not match her own.

Desperate for answers, they returned to the attic. Flipping through the journal, Tommy found a description of a ritual that could supposedly banish the spirits. But it required blood—a sacrifice.

"I'm not doing this!" Allison shouted, backing away. "This is insane!"

Before anyone could argue, the shadows began to close in, whispering louder and more insistent. They could feel the air grow thick with malice, the temperature dropping as the spirits revealed themselves—twisted, half-formed figures, their faces contorted with rage and pain.

They had to act fast.

Tommy grabbed the journal and frantically started reading the incantation. Allison screamed as a shadow lunged at her, wrapping cold, invisible fingers around her throat. Jessica and Tommy tried to free her, but the shadow was too strong. It was as if the house itself was trying to consume her.

The words from the journal echoed through the room, clashing with the furious whispers of the spirits. The walls began to shake, the windows rattled, and the air grew even colder. Jessica could see Mark's face among the shadows, twisted and lost, beckoning them to join him.

The magic wasn't enough. The spirits needed more—they needed a soul. Tommy looked at Jessica, his eyes filled with fear and regret.

"We have to do it," he whispered. "One of us has to stay, or none will leave."

Allison, struggling for breath, nodded weakly. "Go," she rasped. "I'll hold them off. ... go."

Tears filled Jessica's eyes as she and Tommy backed away. Pale but resolute, Allison stood in the center of the room, facing the shadows. As they swarmed over her, the whispers grew into a cacophony.

Tommy and Jessica ran.

They stumbled out of the house, gasping for air, the cold night air feeling like a blessing. They collapsed on the grass, staring up at the manor as the shadows receded into its depths. It was over.

Or so they thought.

As they drove away, the car filled with silence. The town of Draymore lay quiet in the distance, the manor a fading silhouette. But as the wind howled through the trees, Jessica froze. The faintest sound—like whispers—carried on the breeze, growing louder.

The shadows weren't done with them yet.

5

The Return of the Shadows

The nightmares began the day after they escaped the manor. Tommy would wake up in a cold sweat, heart hammering in his chest, his ears filled with faint whispers that he could never quite make out. The house's shadows swirled around him in his dreams, stretching long fingers toward his throat. Sometimes, they spoke in Allison's voice, begging for help, her face distorted and twisted in agony.

Jessica wasn't faring any better. She had stopped returning Tommy's calls. Her health was rapidly deteriorating—her skin pale, her eyes hollow. She hadn't been able to sleep, not really. Every time she closed her eyes, she saw Allison's face, screaming soundlessly, trapped in that house. And worse, she started seeing things in her waking hours, too: shadows flickering across the walls of her apartment, moving even when there was no light to cast them.

At first, she thought she was imagining it. The trauma of their experience at the Crowley manor had to have left scars. But when she heard the whispers in the middle of the night—soft, insistent, calling her name—she knew something was wrong.

Tommy tried to dismiss the occurrences, burying himself in work and drinking away the images that clawed at his mind. But deep down, he knew. The curse hadn't stayed behind. It was with them, growing stronger with every passing day.

It started with small things—doors creaking open, lights flickering, cold drafts in rooms without windows. Tommy blamed faulty wiring, old hinges, and anything rational he could cling to. But the night he saw his kitchen chair move on its own, sliding two feet across the floor with no one near it, he knew he couldn't ignore it any longer.

He called Jessica.

"I can't do this anymore," she whispered, her voice shaking. "They're here, Tommy. The shadows—they followed us. I see them. I hear them. I can't—" Her voice cracked. "It's like they're waiting for something."

Tommy clenched his jaw. "We'll figure this out," he said, though he didn't believe his words. "We'll fix it."

But even as he spoke, the whispers began again, faint and mocking, as though they could sense his fear.

Desperate, Tommy and Jessica sought help. After scouring forums, reading articles about hauntings, and speaking to every local paranormal investigator, they were pointed toward one name: Dr. Evelyn Moore.

Dr. Moore had made a name for herself as an expert in the occult, specializing in hauntings tied to dark rituals. People said she had traveled the world, studying ancient curses and finding ways to break them. Tommy didn't care if the stories were true or exaggerated; he needed answers.

When they met her, she was as intimidating as her reputation suggested. Her gray hair was pulled back into a tight bun, and her piercing blue eyes seemed to look right through them.

"You're both cursed," Dr. Moore said matter-of-factly after hearing their story. "Whatever you encountered in that house—it's latched onto you. Spirits that feed on fear, perhaps. Or something worse."

"What do you mean 'worse'?" Jessica asked, her voice trembling.

Dr. Moore leaned forward, her expression grim. "Spirits are one thing. But if you've awakened something older, something darker, it won't stop until it consumes you. The only way to free yourselves is to finish what was started."

Tommy frowned. "What was started?"

"The spirits are tethered to unfinished business," Dr. Moore explained. "Someone was left behind—Allison. Her soul is trapped there;

unless you return to release her, the shadows will keep growing stronger. They will follow you until they take everything from you."

The idea of returning to Crowley Manor filled them both with dread, but they had no choice. The shadows were becoming bolder, and their presence was suffocating. The whispers grew louder every night, and they could feel the darkness closing in.

They drove to Draymore in silence, the town just as bleak and eerie as they remembered. The locals hadn't forgotten the manor's dark history, either. When Tommy and Jessica entered the small diner in town for a quick bite, the few patrons inside fell silent, staring at them like ghosts.

An older woman leaned over to whisper as they passed, her wrinkled hands clutching a teacup. "Don't go back to that place," she warned, her voice husky. It's not just haunted anymore. It's hungry."

They didn't reply, but the chill in her words stayed with them long after they left the diner.

When they arrived at Crowley Manor's gates, the mansion looked worse. The windows were black and broken in some places, and the roof sagged dangerously. The air around the house seemed to hum with malevolence. It was as if the shadows inside were waiting for them to return.

"This is a bad idea," Jessica muttered, her voice shaky.

"We don't have a choice," Tommy said, gripping the rusted gate. "If we don't go back in there, we're as good as dead."

The moment they stepped through the threshold, the temperature dropped. The house seemed to breathe around them, the walls groaning like the structure was alive. Jessica shivered, clutching her jacket tight around her.

The whispers began almost immediately.

"Help me."

It was Allison's voice, faint but unmistakable. It echoed through the empty halls, calling to them from somewhere deep within the house.

"She's still here," Jessica whispered. "God, she's still here."

They followed the voice, descending deeper into the house. It again led them to the attic, where they had found the cursed journal months ago. But this time, something was different.

A figure stood motionless in the corner of the room, barely visible in the dim light. Jessica gasped, her heart skipping a beat.

"Allison?" she whispered.

The figure turned, and for a brief moment, they saw her face—twisted and worn, her eyes hollow and filled with anguish. Then, she dissolved into the shadows.

Tommy stumbled back, his breath catching in his throat. The shadows swirled around them, growing thicker and darker.

"They're stronger now," Jessica said, her voice trembling. "What do we do?"

Tommy opened his mouth to answer, but before speaking, the attic door slammed shut with a force rattling the walls. The shadows moved in, swirling like a black vortex, surrounding them.

"We finish this," Tommy said, clenching his fists. "We end it, once and for all."

As the shadows closed in, Tommy and Jessica struggled to breathe. The air had thickened as if the darkness itself were choking them. They huddled in the center of the attic, feeling the temperature drop further with every passing second. So many voices echoed around them, blending into a constant, unsettling whisper.

Dr. Evelyn Moore had warned them this would happen. She said the shadows were more than just spirits of the dead—they were ancient, darker, born out of fear and suffering. And now, they were here in full force.

"We need to figure out where Allison's spirit is anchored," Tommy said, his voice shaking but determined. "That's the only way to free her and stop this."

Jessica, pale and trembling, nodded. "But how? She's part of the shadows now. We can't even see her."

The shadows began to take shape before they thought of a plan. Humanoid forms twisted out of the darkness, their features grotesque and distorted, faces frozen in agonized expressions. One of them, taller than the others, stepped forward. Tommy's blood ran cold as the figure's face became more apparent.

It was Mark.

It looked like Mark—or at least, it looked like Mark. His body was a patchwork of shadow and substance, and his eyes were dark pits in his skull. His lips curled into a smile, but it wasn't one of friendliness—it was a predator's grin.

"Miss me?" the shadow figure rasped, its voice low and taunting, an eerie mimicry of their old friend's voice. "You left me behind. Just like you left Allison."

Jessica backed away, her breath hitching. "You're not Mark. You're just one of them."

The figure chuckled, the sound dry and brittle like cracking bones. "Does it matter? I'm part of this house now, just like you will be. You can't leave, Tommy. You can't run. The shadows are everywhere."

Tommy's fists clenched at his sides, anger replacing the fear building inside him. "We didn't leave you behind, Mark. You were already gone. You were one of them."

The shadow figure's smile widened. "We'll see who's left behind this time."

With a sudden burst of movement, the figure lunged toward Jessica, its shadowy hands reaching for her throat. Jessica screamed, stumbling back into Tommy, who pulled her behind him just in time.

"Enough!" a sharp voice rang out through the attic, commanding and powerful.

Dr. Evelyn Moore stood in the doorway, cutting through the oppressive darkness. She held an ancient-looking book in one hand, the pages fluttering open like an unseen wind rifling through them.

"I warned you," Dr. Moore said, her eyes locked on Mark's shadow figure. These shadows are not simple spirits—they are dark entities, older than this house, older than death. They feed on fear, loss, and suffering. And you," she turned her gaze to Tommy and Jessica, "have brought them exactly what they wanted."

The whispering intensified, and the shadows swirled more violently around the room. Dr. Moore's voice grew louder and more robust. "But they can be severed. Their connection to this place can be broken. If we free Allison, they'll lose their power. The darkness cannot thrive without an anchor."

Tommy took a step forward. "Then what are we waiting for? Let's finish this."

Dr. Moore opened her book, flipping through the ancient pages and reading aloud in a language neither Tommy nor Jessica understood. The words were harsh and guttural, yet they seemed to resonate in the air, cutting through the whispers.

The shadows shrieked, recoiling from the sound. Mark's figure writhed, his form flickering between solid and shadow, his voice twisting into a tortured scream.

The attic began to shake, the floorboards groaning under the weight of the evil energy. But something else was happening, too—the shadows were pulling back, retreating toward a single point in the room. Allison's ghostly figure reappeared, standing at the heart of the vortex, her eyes wide and filled with terror.

"We have to free her now!" Jessica shouted over the roar of the shifting shadows.

Dr. Moore quickened her chant, the ancient words echoing in the confined space. But the shadows weren't done. They surged forward again, crashing against the protective barrier the ritual seemed to form around them. Tommy and Jessica clung to each other, eyes wide as the walls around them seemed to bend inward, the darkness pressing in with a nasty hunger.

Suddenly, the attic door slammed shut behind them with a loud crash, sealing them inside. The window shattered inward, spraying shards of glass as the wind outside howled like a wild beast. The darkness moved like a tide, relentless, furious.

Mark's shadow figure reappeared, but he wasn't alone this time. More shadowy figures joined him, their faces unfamiliar but equally twisted and grotesque. Some had once been human, trapped like Allison, but now they were lost to the shadows, their forms distorted beyond recognition. They closed in, their whispers a chorus of torment.

Tommy turned to Dr. Moore. "Can you stop them?"

Dr. Moore's face was tight with concentration. "I can hold them off for a while, but the connection to this place is strong. We need to find where Allison is anchored—something must tie her to the shadows, something from when she was alive."

Tommy's mind raced. "The journal! When we found it, Allison read it just before... before she was taken."

Jessica's eyes widened. "It's still here, in the attic. Maybe it's part of the ritual that binds her."

Dr. Moore nodded. "Find it! But be careful—the shadows will do anything to stop you."

Tommy and Jessica tore through the attic, frantically searching for the journal. Every second felt like an eternity, the oppressive weight of the shadows bearing down on them. They could hear the entities closing in, the sounds of their twisted voices filling the air with threats and promises.

Tommy's flashlight flickered and died, plunging them into darkness. Jessica screamed as one of the shadow figures lunged toward her, but Tommy pulled her away just in time. In the chaos, his foot kicked something heavy—a book.

"The journal!" he shouted, snatching it up.

But the moment his fingers closed around it, the shadows exploded into a frenzy. They screamed in unison, rattling the walls and shaking the house's foundation.

"You've angered them," Dr. Moore said, her voice strained as she continued to chant. "They know you're close to breaking the connection."

Tommy opened the journal with trembling hands to the page where Allison had left her final words. There, in jagged writing, was a single phrase:

"The shadows feed on what we hold onto. My regret, my pain—they keep me here. Free me, and they lose their power."

Tommy's heart pounded as he realized what they had to do. They needed to break Allison's emotional ties to the house—her regret, her pain—before they could sever the shadows' hold on them.

Tommy clutched the journal, his mind racing. Allison's words were clear—her regret and pain were the keys to her imprisonment. The shadows thrived on her emotional torment, and until that was severed, they'd never be free.

"We have to confront her," Tommy said, breathless. "Allison's regret, her pain—it's keeping her here. We need to help her let go."

"How?" Jessica asked, her voice trembling. "She's part of the shadows now."

Dr. Moore stopped her chant momentarily, her eyes narrowing as she glanced at the swirling darkness around them. "There's only one way to force the shadows to release her. You'll have to get through to her—convince her to let go of what's holding her to this world. But be warned: the shadows will do everything they can to keep her trapped."

Tommy swallowed hard. "We can't give up now. We owe this to Allison."

The shadows seemed to sense what they were planning. As they moved deeper into the attic, the dark entities became more aggressive, their forms twisting and writhing with fury. They lashed out at the trio, their cold, phantom hands grazing their skin, but Dr. Moore's chanting kept them at bay, though the strain on her face was becoming more apparent.

Tommy stepped forward, holding the journal tightly. "Allison!" he shouted into the swirling darkness. "We're here! You don't have to stay with them! You can let go—you can be free!"

For a moment, there was silence. Then, Allison's figure slowly reappeared, her ghostly form barely distinguishable from the shadows surrounding her. Her eyes were hollow and filled with pain, and her face was a mask of sorrow.

"I can't leave," she whispered, her voice small and broken. "I made a mistake... I should have listened... but I didn't, and now I'm trapped."

"No," Jessica said, stepping forward. "It wasn't your fault. None of this was your fault. We were all deceived by this place. You don't have to stay here, Allison. You don't have to suffer anymore."

Allison's gaze flickered, and a tear slid down her pale cheek. The shadows around her began to ripple as if sensing her hesitation. Their whispers grew louder and more desperate.

"Stay with us."

"You belong here."

"You can't leave."

The air around them grew colder, more oppressive. Tommy felt the weight of the shadows pressing down on his chest, threatening to suffocate him. "You don't belong here," he shouted, fighting to keep his voice steady. "You can let go of this pain, Allison. You can be at peace."

Allison's face twisted in agony as the shadows tightened around her, pulling her deeper into their dark embrace. "I don't know how to let go," she said, her voice barely audible.

Chanting and faltering as the shadows pressed in, Dr. Moore shouted, "She needs to release her regret! You have to make her see there's nothing left for her here!"

Tears streaming down her face, Jessica reaching out toward Allison's figure. "We forgive you, Allison. It's okay. We all make mistakes. But this place—it's not your prison anymore. You're stronger than the shadows. You can let go."

Allison's form flickered, and the darkness around hewrithedng as if in pain. The shadows screamed in protest, their voices rising in anger and fear. The room shook violently; the walls groaned as if the house were fighting back.

"I'm so sorry," Allison whispered, her voice breaking. "I never wanted any of this. I never wanted to hurt you."

"You didn't hurt us," Tommy said, his voice gentle but firm. "You were a victim, just like we were. It's time to let go, Allison. It's time to be free."

For a moment, the world seemed to stand still. Allison's figure shimmered, her face softening as the torment in her eyes faded. The shadows around her howled in fury, lashing out with desperate fury, but it was too late. Allison's form began to dissolve, her spirit rising above the swirling darkness.

"I'm free," she whispered, a faint smile tugging at the corners of her lips. "Thank you."

And then, she was gone.

The shadows screamed one last time, their forms collapsing into nothingness. The oppressive weight that had filled the attic lifted, and the temperature slowly rose. The darkness receded, pulling away from the walls and corners, retreating into the void from which it had come.

Dr. Moore sighed in relief, her face pale and drawn from the effort of keeping the ritual intact. "It's done," she said, her voice weak but resolute. "The connection is broken."

Tommy and Jessica stood in the attic ruins, the oppressive darkness finally gone. The house was eerily silent now; the whispers that had tormented them for so long were gone with Allison's release.

"We did it," Jessica said, her voice barely above a whisper.

Tommy nodded, though the victory felt hollow. They had freed Allison, but the cost had been significant. The house had taken so much from them—Mark and Allison—and the trauma of what they had experienced would never truly leave them.

Dr. Moore wiped the sweat from her brow, closing the ancient book she had used to sever the curse. "You're both lucky to be alive," she said, her tone serious. "Most people who encounter shadows this old don't make it out."

As they made their way out of the house, the oppressive weight lifted further. Outside, the sky was a bright, cloudless blue, as if the darkness that had once suffocated the manor had finally released its grip. Tommy and Jessica breathed in the fresh air, feeling a sense of relief they hadn't known in months.

"I can't believe it's over," Jessica said, her voice shaky but filled with hope.

But just as they reached the edge of the property, something made Tommy stop. He glanced back at the crumbling manor, its windows shattered and dark, its roof sagging like an ancient beast finally defeated.

For a moment, all was still.

But then he saw a flicker in one of the upper windows. A shadow, brief but unmistakable. It moved too fast to register fully, but he knew what he had seen.

A faint whisper brushed past his ear.

"You can never leave..."

Tommy's blood ran cold. His face was pale, and he turned to Jessica. "Did you hear that?"

She frowned. "Hear what?"

Tommy swallowed hard, glancing back at the house one last time. "Nothing," he said, though the unease gnawed at his insides. He turned away, but the faint whisper lingered in his mind.

Had they truly escaped the shadows? Or was the curse still waiting, biding its time?

As they walked away from the manor, Tommy couldn't shake the feeling that the shadows were watching... waiting for their chance to return.

6

The Eternal Shadows

Months had passed since Tommy and Jessica left Crowley Manor. They thought they were free—that Allison's release had broken the curse. But the shadows had never indeed left.

Tommy was now living in a small apartment, far from Draymore, trying to piece his life back together. But the nightmares continued. The shadows visited him in his sleep, dark tendrils creeping across his mind. No matter where he went, the feeling of being watched never left him.

Jessica had moved in with her sister across the country, hoping that distance would sever the connection to the cursed house. For a while, she managed to find some peace. But one night, she heard the whisper while alone in her room.

"You can never leave..."

It was faint, barely noticeable, but it sent chills down her spine. At first, she dismissed it as her mind playing tricks on her. But the shadows returned, growing stronger with each passing night. They no longer stayed in the corners of her vision—they followed her, always lurking just out of sight.

Tommy and Jessica reunited when the nightmares became unbearable, their shared experience bonding them in ways they couldn't escape. They sought out Dr. Evelyn Moore again, but she wasn't surprised to see them this time. Her once stoic expression had darkened.

"I feared this would happen," she said, her voice low. "The shadows—what you encountered at Crowley Manor—were merely manifestations of something far older and more dangerous."

Tommy frowned. "What do you mean?"

Dr. Moore pulled out a map, tracing a line across several locations, each marked with dates back centuries. "The shadows are part of an ancient force that predates the house, predates even human history. It's been dormant for centuries, feeding off fear and tragedy, but something has awakened it."

Jessica stared at the map, her eyes wide. "Are you saying Crowley Manor was just one of many places haunted by this... thing?"

Dr. Moore nodded grimly. "The house was merely a conduit, a vessel for the larger entity. It thrives in places of pain and death, slowly growing stronger until it can manifest fully in our world."

Tommy felt a chill creep up his spine. "So, what happened to us... it's not over?"

"No," Dr. Moore said. "The entity has attached itself to you both. It used the manor to begin its work, but now that the house has been emptied of its spirits, it seeks to move beyond. It needs you to complete its resurrection."

After leaving Dr. Moore's house, Tommy and Jessica could no longer deny the reality they faced. The shadows were more than mere hauntings; they were part of a force beyond human comprehension. And now, they were marked.

The shadows were growing bolder. They no longer waited for nightfall—they appeared in reflections, in the spaces between moments, in every dark corner. The whispers grew louder, more insistent, but they weren't pleading like before. Now, they were threatening.

One night, Tommy woke up to find the shadows standing at the foot of his bed. They were no longer formless entities. They had faces—Mark, Allison, and other tortured souls they didn't recognize—but their expressions were twisted into grotesque masks of rage. The figures spoke as one:

"You belong to us now."

The room shook, the temperature plummeting as the shadows grew closer. Tommy could barely move, the weight of their presence suffocating him. But then, as suddenly as they appeared, they vanished, leaving only the faint echo of their whispers in his ears.

The following day, Tommy found a mark on his arm—an intricate, swirling design that pulsed with a strange energy. Jessica had the same mark. The shadows had claimed them.

Desperate for answers, Tommy and Jessica returned to Dr. Moore. The older woman, pale and haggard from sleepless nights, explained the true extent of their predicament.

"There's a ritual," Dr. Moore said, her voice barely above a whisper. "A ritual that can sever the connection between you and the entity. But it's more dangerous than anything you've faced before."

Jessica leaned forward. "What do we need to do?"

Dr. Moore hesitated. "The ritual requires confronting the entity on its terms. It would be best to travel to a place where the veil between our world and the shadow realm is thinnest. You'll have to force the entity to reveal its true form there. Only then can you banish it."

"And where is this place?" Tommy asked, his voice thick with dread.

Dr. Moore's eyes darkened. "Back where it all began—Crowley Manor. The house may be empty, but the land itself is tainted. The shadows are tied to the place, and you can only face the entity head-on."

Tommy and Jessica didn't want to return, but they had no choice. Armed with Dr. Moore's instructions and the ritual that could potentially save them, they made the fateful drive to Crowley Manor one last time.

The house was even more decayed than before. The roof had collapsed in some places, and the windows were broken, like dark eyes staring into their souls. The air around the property felt heavier, as if the shadows were waiting for their return.

Inside the house, the temperature dropped instantly. The walls seemed to breathe, pulsing with an unnatural energy. The shadows were everywhere now, flickering in and out of sight, watching them.

"We have to start the ritual now," Jessica said, her voice shaky but determined.

They made their way to the heart of the house, where the ritual was to take place. In the center of the room, they drew the sigils Dr. Moore had instructed, using candles and symbols that pulsed with an eerie light.

As they began the chant, the house shook violently, and shadows swirled around them like a storm. The air became thick with malevolent energy, and the whispers grew louder and distorted.

"You cannot escape."

"We are eternal."

The room was filled with darkness, but this time, it was different. The shadows began to coalesce into a single form, a towering figure of pure darkness, its eyes burning with malevolent intent. This was the entity—ancient, powerful, and filled with rage.

Tommy's heart raced as he locked eyes with the creature. This was the thing that had been haunting them, the force behind the curse. The ritual was their only hope, but the entity was more substantial than they'd imagined.

The air in Crowley Manor vibrated with dark energy as the entity took form, its towering shadow filling the room. Its eyes glowed an eerie red, and its shape was more horrifying than either Tommy or Jessica could have imagined. It wasn't just a ghost or a malevolent spirit—it was something far older, a being that had existed long before human fears gave it form.

The sigils on the floor flickered, struggling to hold back the entity's presence. The candles around the room flared violently as the ancient words of the ritual echoed in the oppressive space.

Tommy's throat was dry as he began reciting the next part of the incantation, his voice shaking but resolute. Jessica stood beside him, clutching the journal and watching the entity with wide eyes. Every instinct in her body screamed at her to run, but she knew there was no escape.

The entity's form began to ripple, the darkness swirling more violently around them. It leaned closer, its voice booming like thunder.

"You think your pitiful ritual will save you? I am eternal. You are nothing but fleeting shadows yourselves."

The sheer weight of the being's voice made the walls tremble, cracks spider-webbing across the ceiling. But they continued, refusing to let the fear take hold.

As Tommy chanted the final verse of the ritual, the entity let out a roar that shook the entire house. The shadowy tendrils lashed out, trying to extinguish the candles and break the protective circle, but the sigils flared brightly in response, holding the darkness at bay.

For a moment, the entity seemed to falter. The shadows recoiled, writhing as if in pain. The glowing red eyes dimmed slightly, and a low hiss of frustration escaped its dark form.

"We're weakening it!" Jessica shouted over the roar of the collapsing house. "Keep going!"

But as they pressed on, the entity's form suddenly stabilized. Its eyes blazed brighter than before, and it let out a terrible, guttural laugh.

"You cannot banish me. Your rituals do not bind me. Your suffering has already given me strength beyond your comprehension."

The room twisted, the very space around them warping. Suddenly, the shadows surged forward, knocking Tommy to the ground. His voice faltered, and the incantation broke. The protective sigils flickered, then went out.

Jessica screamed as the darkness enveloped them. The entity loomed over Tommy, its shadowy hands extending toward him.

The darkness swirled around Tommy, cold and suffocating. He struggled to breathe as the entity's hand drew closer, its fingers like tendrils of smoke ready to snuff out his life. Jessica scrambled to reach him, but the shadows wrapped around her ankles, pulling her back.

Tommy's mind raced. The ritual wasn't enough. The entity had grown too powerful from years of feeding on the pain and suffering of its victims. They needed something more to weaken its grip on them once and for all.

Then it hit him. The mark. The swirling, glowing pattern on his arm—the one the entity had left on them both. The entity had branded them, connected them to its dark essence. And that connection went both ways.

Tommy grabbed Jessica's hand and shouted, "The mark! It's a link between us and the entity! If we can sever it, we can break free!"

Jessica's eyes widened in realization. The connection worked like a rope, binding them to the entity and allowing them to fight back. They might have a chance if they could turn the entity's power against itself.

Together, they focused on the marks, willing them to burn bright. The entity roared in fury as the marks on their arms began to glow with an intense light, more colorful and more robust than before. The darkness around them recoiled, and the entity's form destabilized.

"You think you can break my hold?" the entity hissed, its voice shaking with rage. "I am beyond you. I am—"

Before it could finish, Tommy and Jessica concentrated on the marks with every ounce of strength they had left. The glowing light intensified, filling the room with a blinding brilliance that cut through the shadows. The entity howled in agony, its form flickering violently.

The marks on their arms flared brighter, the connection between them and the entity severing with a snap. The shadows screamed as the link was broken, and the entity's form unraveled. Its towering figure collapsed in on itself, the darkness swirling into a vortex of shadow and fury.

With a final, earth-shaking roar, the entity was pulled back into the void, disappearing into the abyss from which it had come.

The moment the entity vanished, the oppressive weight lifted from the room. The candles flickered back to life, casting a warm, gentle glow. The air, which had been thick with dread, was now still. The house was silent.

Tommy and Jessica sat on the floor, breathing heavily, their bodies aching from the effort. The marks on their arms were gone, leaving only faint scars as a reminder of what had just transpired.

For a long time, they didn't speak. The silence felt alien after the chaos they had just endured, but it was a welcome relief. The shadows were gone, the entity was gone, and they felt free for the first time in months.

"It's over," Jessica whispered, her voice shaky.

Tommy nodded, though he still couldn't quite believe it. The terror of Crowley Manor, the entity, and the shadows felt like a nightmare that had finally ended.

They stood slowly, looking around the decaying room. The house was no longer alive with malevolent energy. It was just a house now—broken, decaying, but no longer haunted.

"We should get out of here," Tommy said, offering Jessica a hand.

She took it, and together, they made their way out of the house. The sunlight outside was blinding after so long in the darkness, but it felt good. The weight of the past months, the terror they had faced, slowly began to lift from their shoulders.

Tommy and Jessica struggled to adjust to everyday life in the following days. The scars from their ordeal ran deep, and though the entity was gone, the memories of what they had faced were not so easily forgotten.

They contacted Dr. Moore, who reassured them that the ritual had worked. The entity's connection to them had been severed, and without the shadows to sustain it, it had been banished back to whatever dark realm it had come from.

But despite her reassurances, Tommy couldn't shake the feeling that something was still watching them. Now and then, in the quiet moments of the night, he thought he heard faint whispers, just at the edge of hearing. He told himself it was just his imagination, the lingering effects of the trauma.

Jessica had nightmares, too, but they were less frequent as time passed. They both tried to move on, to leave the horrors of Crowley Manor behind. But the experience had changed them in ways they couldn't fully understand.

Months later, Tommy stood frozen in his apartment, his heart pounding as the chilling whispers filled the air. The shadows in the corner shifted ominously, and the weight of dread pressed down on him. But he refused to let fear control him again.

"You cannot escape..." The voice echoed, dark and twisted.

Drawing a deep breath, Tommy steeled himself. He remembered the ritual and the strength he and Jessica had found in each other. This time, he would not succumb to despair. He would confront whatever lingered in the shadows.

"Get out!" he shouted, his voice strong and clear. "You have no power over me!"

The shadows flickered and writhed as if in response, but the whispers grew quieter, more uncertain. Tommy took a step forward, determination surging within him. "You were defeated. You have no hold on me or Jessica!"

The shadows recoiled, but he could feel their anger radiating from the dark corner. Tommy summoned the memory of the ritual, the warmth of the light that had banished the entity, and called upon that strength again. "You are nothing but a remnant, a fading echo. I refuse to be your puppet!"

With every word, he felt the connection between them weaken. The shadows writhed more violently, and the whispers transformed into howls of fury. But Tommy held his ground, drawing power from the scars on his arm, which pulsed with a renewed glow.

"Jessica!" he called, knowing she would be there for him, even if she were miles away. "I need you!"

At that moment, the shadows darkened, then suddenly burst into a brilliant light, illuminating the room and revealing a swirling vortex of darkness at its center. Tommy felt a surge of energy, a tether connecting him to Jessica, who was fighting her battles.

The darkness in the vortex swirled more violently, and Tommy realized this was the final confrontation. He could end it here, once and for all. He reached deep within himself, grasping the strength of their shared experience and the love that had brought them together.

"By the light of our bond, I banish you!" he shouted, and with those words, he pushed the light from the marks on his arm into the darkness.

The shadows screamed, and the vortex began to close in on itself, struggling against Tommy's radiant resolve. With a final, powerful surge, he felt the entity being pulled away, its form unraveling as the light engulfed it.

"Be gone!" Tommy roared, channeling every ounce of willpower he had left.

With one last howl of fury, the darkness shattered, dissolving into a brilliant light that filled the room. The oppressive energy lifted, and Tommy felt a true sense of peace over him for the first time.

Epilogue: A New Dawn

Days later, Tommy stood outside his apartment, watching the sunrise. The sky was painted with hues of orange and pink, a stark contrast to the darkness he had faced. He felt lighter; the weight of the shadows finally lifted.

Jessica called him that morning, her voice filled with warmth. "How are you holding up?"

"I think I'm okay," Tommy replied, a smile breaking through his anxiety. "I faced the darkness last night. I confronted it, and it's finally gone."

"That's incredible! I knew you could do it," Jessica said, her voice brimming with pride. "We're free now, Tommy. Truly free."

As they talked, Tommy glanced toward Crowley Manor in the distance. The house stood silent, no longer a beacon for the shadows. He knew their experience's scars would linger, but they were finally free from the entity's grasp.

With Jessica by his side, he felt hopeful about the future. They could rebuild their lives, leaving the horrors of the past behind.

Tommy took a deep breath, feeling the sun's warmth on his skin, the whispers of the past fading away.

As the new day began, he knew the shadows would never return. They had faced their fears and emerged stronger. This time, they had indeed escaped.

7

The Perfect Selfie

The wind howled as Claire stood at the edge of Raven's Peak, a towering cliff that overlooked miles of jagged rocks and an unforgiving sea. It was a popular spot for hikers and thrillers, and Claire had always dreamed of visiting. After months of planning, she was finally here, standing at the precipice of one of the most dangerous cliffs in the country.

But she wasn't here for the view...at least, not in the traditional sense. Claire was here for the perfect selfie.

Her social media presence has exploded in recent months, and her daring photos and adventurous spirit have garnered thousands of followers. She has climbed mountains, crossed rickety rope bridges, and snapped pictures in the wildest locations, but nothing compares to the deadly beauty of Raven's Peak.

She could already see it in her mind: a perfectly angled shot of her standing triumphantly against the backdrop of the infinite sky and crashing waves below...the ultimate post.

The warnings didn't matter to her. Everyone knew Raven's Peak was dangerous. The locals had a name for it: The Cliff of Lost Souls. Dozens of people had died there; their bodies never recovered from the turbulent waters below. But to Claire, the name was just part of the allure.

She set up her phone on a small tripod and backed toward the cliff's edge, glancing over her shoulder to ensure she had enough of the jagged drop in the frame. The cold wind whipped her hair across her face, and the sun began to set, casting an eerie glow on the horizon. It was perfect.

The sky looked like it was on fire, a blaze of reds and oranges that contrasted with the dark rocks below. This was it... shot would cement her as a social media icon.

"Just a little further back," she muttered, stepping closer to the edge.

The rocks beneath her feet were loose, and the cliff's edge was uneven. A slight, unsettling crunch echoed as her boot scraped against the stones. But Claire was focused, too intent on the picture to care. She leaned back slightly, ensuring her face, the cliff, and the sky fit perfectly in the frame.

As the phone's timer counted down, Claire glanced up. For a split second, her heart skipped a beat. She thought she saw a shadow figure behind her in the phone's reflection. But when she turned around, there was nothing but the emptiness of the cliffside.

The timer beeped. The phone captured the shot.

Claire grinned, stepping forward to check her photo. But as she moved, the ground beneath her gave way with a sickening crack. In an instant, the earth crumbled under her feet, and her body tilted backward, arms flailing as she tried to grab hold of anything...anything...to stop her fall.

The howling wind swallowed her scream as she plunged into the abyss below. The world blurred into a spinning mass of sky, cliff, and ocean. The jagged rocks below loomed more extensive with each passing second, and then...

Blackness.

Claire awoke to silence.

She lay on something cold and challenging, but the pain she expected never came. Groggily, she sat up, her vision swimming. She was still on the cliff, but something was wrong. The sky was dark, the stars cold and distant, and the wind, once fierce, was now eerily still. Her phone was lying on the ground beside her, its screen cracked but still lit. The photo she had taken before her fall was open on the screen.

But as Claire looked closer, her blood ran cold. In the photo, she wasn't alone.

A figure cloaked in shadow stood behind her in the picture. Its face was obscured, but its eyes glowed a sickly yellow. The figure's outstretched hand seemed to rest on Claire's shoulder as if pulling her toward the edge.

A cold dread gripped her chest as she scrambled to her feet, glancing around wildly. The cliff was deserted, but the oppressive feeling of being watched crept over her like a suffocating blanket.

Then she heard it...a whisper. Soft at first, barely audible over her racing heartbeat.

"Come closer..."

Claire froze. The voice was distant yet intimate, as though it came from the very ground beneath her. She spun around, eyes scanning the cliff for any movement. Nothing. But the whisper grew louder.

"Come to me..."

Her breath caught in her throat as she backed away from the edge. But with every step she took, the whisper seemed to grow more insistent, filling her mind with a buzzing pressure that made it impossible to think.

Suddenly, her phone screen flickered, and the photo changed. Now, the shadowy figure in the picture was moving—its head slowly turning to face her, its glowing eyes locking onto hers.

Claire's phone slipped from her hand and shattered against the rocks.

She turned to run, but her body wouldn't obey. It was as if invisible hands were holding her in place, dragging her closer to the cliff's edge. She tried to scream, but no sound escaped her lips. Her heart raced, each beat echoing in her ears as the ground beneath her shifted again, crumbling away like sand.

Then she saw...figures...rising from the rocks below. Their faint, ghostly outlines were undeniable, but their presence was unmistakable. Dozens of them...the Lost Souls of Raven's Peak—glowed in the darkness; their hollow eyes shone, and their gaunt, spectral faces twisted with agony.

They reached for her, their transparent hands grasping the air and pulling her toward them. The whisper grew deafening, and a symphony of voices filled her mind.

"Join us..."

Claire struggled, but it was no use. The pull was too strong. Her feet slid toward the edge, her body moving against her will. She could feel the cold, clammy touch of the Lost Souls as they latched onto her, dragging her down, down, down into the abyss.

Her last thought before the darkness swallowed her was that she had finally become part of the perfect shot.

The next day, hikers found Claire's phone shattered on the rocks at the edge of Raven's Peak. There was no sign of her body, just an empty void where she had once stood.

The only clue was the final photo on her phone...a haunting image of Claire smiling at the cliff's edge. But behind her, barely visible in the shadows, was the figure of a man. His glowing eyes stared into the camera, his hand resting on Claire's shoulder.

The legend of Raven's Peak grew that day.

They say the cliff claims those who come too close, luring them in with promises of the perfect selfie. But once you take that picture, the Lost Souls reach out from the abyss, pulling you into their world...forever.

8

A Halloween to Remember

The little town of Willow's Hollow had always held an air of mystery, especially during Halloween, and this year, the holiday promised to be even spookier with the arrival of the mysterious Eldridge family. They had moved into the old mansion on Ravenswood Lane, long rumored to be haunted. As the townspeople whispered about strange happenings and the odd lights coming from the mansion, young Jenny, Tom, and Liam decided they had to see for themselves. With Halloween night approaching, the friends made a pact to investigate.

Halloween night came, and as trick-or-treaters filled the streets, the trio snuck toward the Eldridge mansion. Clutching flashlights, they pushed open the creaky gate and stepped into the overgrown garden. Jenny noticed an odd symbol carved into the wood of the front door, and Liam claimed he heard a faint whisper. Despite their nerves, they went inside, finding the mansion dark and silent. As they explored, they discovered hidden passages, eerie paintings, and peculiar artifacts that hinted at secrets older than the town itself.

Leaving the mansion unsettled but alive, the three returned to the neighborhood, only to find it transformed. The streets were cloaked in dense fog, and the trick-or-treaters had vanished. The trio tried to head home, but they couldn't shake the feeling that something was watching them. Suddenly, shadows shifted in the fog, and strange figures appeared—children in tattered costumes with vacant eyes, eerily silent and still. The haunted Halloween was only beginning.

The friends sought refuge in an old cemetery near the mansion as the ghostly children began following them. There, they met someone unexpected: a boy their age named Elias, who wore an old-fashioned suit and claimed he knew the mansion's history and curse. According to Elias, a Halloween night occurs every hundred years when the line between the living and the dead is blurred in Willow's Hollow. The Eldridges were caretakers of this "Night of the Spirits" and had unwittingly released the ancient curse. The entire town would be trapped in an endless Halloween nightmare if it wasn't stopped.

With a new goal, the friends and Elias set off to find the Eldridges and break the curse. As they ventured deeper into the fog, they faced strange illusions: familiar places turned twisted and grotesque, and their worst fears seemed to come to life around them. Visions of a lost family member haunted Tom, while Jenny saw monstrous versions of herself. Liam nearly froze in fear as disembodied voices whispered his name. They had to stay together and push forward, resisting the growing terror around them.

After nearly giving up, they finally found the Eldridges in the mansion's library, surrounded by spellbooks and glowing artifacts. Mr. Eldridge explained that he had been trying to contain the curse, but it had become too powerful. As the spirits of Halloween past gathered strength, they began to breach the protective barriers of the mansion. The only way to stop the curse, he revealed, was for someone brave enough to retrieve an amulet hidden in the oldest tomb in the graveyard—a place most feared in Willow's Hollow.

Armed with a map provided by Mrs. Eldridge, the group headed to the tomb, its iron doors bound with ancient chains. As they pried the doors open, strange shadows crept along the walls, whispering the names of each child. Inside, they found the tomb covered in dust, with an ominous, glowing amulet lying in the center. Elias reached for it, but the amulet lashed out with dark energy, and Jenny barely caught him as he stumbled back. They realized that the amulet required something in return for its power: courage, hope, and the willingness to face their deepest fears.

Each friend had to confront a personal fear to lift the curse. Liam went first, battling his fear of being abandoned in an endless void. Jenny then faced her fear of losing herself to the darkness, while Tom was forced to confront a guilt that had haunted him for years. When each had proven their courage, the amulet glowed brightly, signaling that the curse was weakening. But Elias, with a mysterious sadness, stepped forward last, knowing he, too, must face his fear of leaving the earthly realm.

With the amulet in hand, they raced back to the Eldridge mansion, only to find it surrounded by eerie spirits trapped between life and death. They hurried inside and presented the amulet to Mr. Eldridge, who began a ritual to reverse the curse. Just as the clock struck midnight, a powerful wave of energy erupted from the amulet, sweeping across the town and banishing the spirits back to the afterlife. Elias, who had helped the friends from beyond, faded into the fog with a bittersweet smile.

The fog lifted, and the children of Willow's Hollow returned home safely, oblivious to the supernatural events that had unfolded. The trio, forever bonded by their experience, kept their adventure a secret, knowing few would believe them. The Eldridge family remained in Willow's Hollow, guardians of the town's forgotten history. And every Halloween, Jenny, Tom, and Liam would place a small candle on Elias's grave, remembering the friend who had helped them survive a Halloween no one else would ever forget.

That Halloween in Willow's Hollow was now the stuff of legend, a haunting tale that would be whispered for generations.

9

Echoes in the Dark

John Paul's story begins in a forgotten small town shrouded in perpetual mist, where he arrives with excitement and dread. He meets with a peculiar old lawyer, Mr. Crane, who knows more than he lets on about the legacy John Paul is set to inherit. Mr. Crane's eyes glint with something unreadable as he hands over an ancient key and a sealed letter left by his uncle, which John Paul is instructed not to open until he's in the mansion.

The mansion looms on the edge of the town, concealed by towering oaks that cast eerie shadows. The structure is an oppressive Victorian monstrosity with turrets and cracked windows. The interior feels claustrophobic, dark, and hostile. Dust motes drift in the stagnant air, and the smell of decay clings to every surface as he explores the rooms; a strange tension builds as though each step disturbs an unseen presence. He hears faint, nearly imperceptible whispers, and in certain rooms, it's as if the shadows shift when he isn't looking. Despite his reservations, John Paul decides to stay, lured by the mystery of the place—and perhaps by the allure of finally learning more about his enigmatic family history.

Just before drifting off that night, he feels a strange sensation—a slight, icy breeze caresses his face as though someone is breathing near him. He jolts awake but finds only darkness around him.

Haunted by strange dreams of labyrinthine hallways and chanting voices, John Paul feels drained and uneasy the following day. Determined to explore, he stumbles upon a locked room at the end of a narrow, dark corridor, nearly hidden behind old, dusty curtains. The door is strangely cold, and when he touches it, an electric sensation jolts through his fingers. He spends hours searching the mansion for a key, finally finding one hidden in a hollow book inside the library—a leather-bound tome with no title.

He unlocks the door, stepping into an eerie, dimly lit chamber dominated by a massive, wall-length mirror encased in an ornate, gilded frame. The mirror's surface is dark, almost black, and when he looks into it, his reflection seems... off. It's not just a delay; it's as if his reflection is reacting to something else in the room, something John Paul can't see. As he approaches, he feels a deep, pulsing vibration, and a faint whisper reaches his ears—a language he doesn't understand but which fills him with intense dread.

In the corner of the room, he finds an old journal wrapped in cracked leather. Written in his uncle's handwriting, it mentions rituals, "the veil," and cryptic references to "The Dweller in the Mirror." John Paul tries to leave but hears his name faintly called from within the mirror. Frightened, he shuts the door and bolts it, but the sensation of being watched lingers as he walks away.

Eager to understand his family's mysterious past, John Paul ventures into town, where he visits the local library and speaks with townsfolk. As he digs through historical records, he finds news clippings and documents about his uncle—Henry St. Claire, an eccentric scholar who had once been a respected academic before seemingly vanished from society. Rumors circulate about his obsession with the occult and his attempts to make contact with "the other side." John Paul learns his uncle purchased the mansion after a personal tragedy, but no one knows precisely what happened.

One particularly haunting story stands out: the townspeople claim that many who entered the house didn't come back out over the years. Several servants had quit suddenly, and one young maid was said to have gone mad, claiming she'd seen her death in the mansion's mirror. Another elderly resident recalls when his uncle was said to have had strange visitors—people who seemed "not of this world" and who left weird markings on the ground near the mansion.

That night, John Paul returns to the mansion, his mind filled with growing dread. As he falls asleep, the whispers grow louder. He dreams of a dark figure watching him from a window, but each time he tries to move, he feels paralyzed, trapped in place by an unseen force.

John Paul's fixation with the mirror grows. Each day, he's drawn to the locked room as if in a trance, compelled to stare into the dark glass. He sees things within its depths—shadows flit across, and at times, the reflection of the room behind him appears distorted, as if he's glimpsing an alternate reality. One evening, he catches a reflection of himself with a twisted, ghastly smile, his eyes filled with something dark and evil. He stumbles back, his heart pounding, but the image is gone as quickly as it appeared.

Over the following nights, his dreams grow increasingly disturbing. He sees himself tortured, engulfed in flames, or sinking into a bottomless pit, each dream accompanied by the sight of himself watching from the mirror, emotionless and unblinking. He tries to avoid the room but finds himself unable to resist. The mirror's pull strengthens each night, and his reflection grows more twisted each time.

Eventually, he realizes that the mirror isn't just showing him nightmares—it's feeding off his fear, amplifying his anxiety, and slowly wearing down his sanity. Desperate, he tries covering it with a cloth, but in the morning, he finds the fabric burnt to a crisp, the mirror untouched.

Soon, the entire house seems to come alive. John Paul begins hearing soft, taunting voices from inside the walls, following him from room to room. The voices start as faint whispers but grow louder each night, chanting phrases he can barely comprehend, phrases that sound like pleas, curses, and warnings all at once. In some rooms, the wallpaper seems to undulate as though breathing, and the floorboards creak in rhythmic pulses, almost as if they're following him.

One night, the voices reach a crescendo, and John Paul hears a distinct, bloodcurdling scream that reverberates through the entire mansion. He rushes to the source, only to find his reflection, contorted in agony, staring back at him from the mirror's depths. In panic, he scratches at the wallpaper and sees something chilling: blood-red markings beneath, forming strange symbols.

Shaken, he retreats to his room, where he finds a message scrawled in the dust on his desk: FIND THE BASEMENT. His heart races as he realizes the house is guiding him to something hidden and terrible.

Part 2:

With mounting dread, John Paul scours the mansion for the basement. After a day of searching, he lifts a dusty, tattered carpet in the study and finds a trapdoor. As he opens it, a rush of cold air greets him, and he sees steep, narrow steps leading into darkness.

The basement is far more extensive than expected, a sprawling network of narrow passageways and hidden nooks. Dim, flickering lanterns cast long shadows, revealing the remnants of his uncle's experiments. Shelves are filled with grotesque relics—preserved animal parts, strange jars with ominous symbols, and yellowed books filled with cryptic passages in languages John Paul can't understand.

He finds a journal that describes his uncle's descent into madness. His uncle believed he had found a way to bridge the human world with a shadow realm, using the mirror as a conduit. His uncle attempted to summon something—a dark entity that could grant knowledge and power but at a terrible price. The pact involved a sacrifice—something precious, but the details are obscured by smeared ink. John Paul realizes he's inherited this cursed pact and that the mansion's hauntings are part of a ritual meant to claim him, body and soul.

One night, John Paul awakens in what appears to be a distorted version of the mansion. The walls pulse with dark energy, and everything around him seems wrong—doors shift locations, mirrors reflect only shadows, and every room leads into an endless maze. He realizes he's not just dreaming; he's been pulled into a nightmare realm—a liminal space controlled by the entity within the mirror. He is confronted by visions of his past sins, fears, and failures everywhere he turns. Faceless figures with elongated, spindly limbs chase him, whispering in familiar voices. Each time he attempts to escape, he returns to the mirror, where his reflection grins with malice. Exhausted, he finally collapses in front of the mirror, whispering a desperate plea to be freed.

After another night of relentless hauntings, John Paul retreats to his uncle's study. The whispering has become a constant, insidious presence; the voices no longer fade even during daylight hours, and darkened reflections seem to follow him outside the mirror room. Poring over the cracked journal and the ancient texts he found in the basement, he begins piecing together the twisted legacy left by his uncle, Henry St. Claire, and the demonic entity within the mirror.

Through fragments of letters, notes, and cryptic Latin passages, John Paul discovers that his uncle had once been a brilliant scholar of ancient languages, exceptionally versed in dead languages referencing supernatural realms. After the loss of a close family member, Henry became obsessed with contacting the dead, and it was this obsession that led him to purchase the mansion. He intended to use the house as a laboratory to channel energies from "the other side." Over time, Henry had become involved in dangerous occult rituals, eventually forging a pact with a creature he called "The Dweller." This entity, bound to the mansion through the mirror, promised Henry glimpses into a hidden world, power beyond mortal comprehension, and the preservation of his spirit beyond death.

The specifics of the pact are chilling. John Paul learns that "The Dweller" operates by binding itself to reflective surfaces. It sustains itself by feeding off the fear and torment of those it traps. In exchange for eternal life within the mirror, Henry agreed to offer a sacrifice—his bloodline. Over the years, Henry would invite family members to visit, luring them into the house's supernatural grasp and letting the creature consume their terror.

But the pact didn't end with Henry's death; instead, it passed to the next of kin. Each heir was "chosen" by the mirror, continuing the cycle unless they managed to break the curse. Reading this, John Paul's hands tremble. He's horrified by the thought that he, too, is intended to become another offering. As he delves further into his uncle's notes, he finds a ritual designed to sever the pact—but the text is smeared and incomplete, hinting that the ritual carries a deadly risk. John Paul begins to wonder if the curse can be broken or if he's trapped in a game his uncle never intended to win.

As night falls, John Paul feels the mansion's walls closing in on him, thick with shadows. The mirror has become more than an object; it's a conscious force, amplifying his fear and testing his resolve. Exhausted and terrified, John Paul decides to proceed with the ritual. He realizes that destroying the mirror might be his only way out, even if it means confronting the full wrath of the being inside.

John Paul spends the following day preparing for the ritual, gathering items specified in the journal: salt, candles, an iron hammer, and a bowl of blessed water. He arranges them in a protective circle around the mirror room, as the journal indicates that binding the mirror within a "salt ring" is crucial to containing The Dweller's power. The sense of dread in the house intensifies as he works; shadows seem to thicken, and strange sounds echo through the halls. Despite the daylight, the mansion is shrouded in darkness, as though the house itself is trying to prevent him from breaking free.

At midnight, John Paul lights the candles and begins chanting an incantation from the journal. He feels an intense pressure as the words leave his lips, as though each syllable weighs down his soul. The mirror's surface ripples, and John Paul can see his uncle's face emerging from the darkness. His reflection is distorted, his eyes hollow, but his expression is filled with rage and despair. His uncle's voice joins John Paul's in a cacophony of whispers, chanting in unison, warning him to stop, begging him to run.

As John Paul continues, the mirror pulses with dark energy, and The Dweller begins to manifest. Its silhouette emerges, flickering in and out of sight, a twisted, monstrous figure with limbs that seem too long and eyes that are nothing but dark pits. It snarls and hisses, reverberating through the room and shaking the walls. The entity's voice joins the chanting, warping the words, twisting them, trying to disrupt the ritual. The salt around the mirror begins to dissolve, and a dark mist seeps from the edges, curling toward John Paul. He feels an unbearable chill, as if the air is being sucked out of his lungs.

Just as he reaches the climax of the magic, the creature lunges at him from within the mirror. John Paul raises the hammer, smashing it against the glass with all his strength. The mirror splinters but doesn't shatter completely; instead, it fractures, creating a dozen distorted reflections of his face, each filled with terror. The Dweller shrieks, its voice like nails on glass, and the room fills with a blinding light. Shadows spiral around him, clawing at his skin and tearing at his clothes, trying to drag him into the mirror's fractured depths.

Summoning every ounce of courage, John Paul repeatedly strikes the mirror with each blow, the glass splinters further, releasing cold, sickly air bursts. The Dweller's form dissipates, its shrieks blending with his uncle's voice. Finally, the mirror shatters completely with one last swing, sending shards flying across the room. The candles flicker out, and a deafening silence fills the air as the entity vanishes, leaving only a hollow, echoing silence in its wake.

In the aftermath, John Paul collapses, barely able to breathe, his hands shaking uncontrollably. The mansion is eerily silent, as though in shock. But the oppressive energy that once filled every room is gone, and the presence that lurked within the walls has vanished. For the first time, John Paul feels a sense of peace, yet he can't shake the lingering sensation of being watched, as though fragments of The Dweller remain hidden within the shattered pieces of the mirror.

He slowly walks through the mansion, stumbling over broken furniture and debris, feeling like he's emerging from a nightmare. Outside, the first light of dawn begins to break through the trees, casting a gentle glow over the house. He glances back at the mansion; its once ominous aura has faded, replaced by a hollow, haunting silence.

But as he steps outside, he's met by several townsfolk who have gathered around the property. They stare at him with expressions of both pity and horror, some muttering prayers, others whispering stories of previous heirs who tried to break the curse. John Paul realizes that the townspeople had always known about the mansion's dark legacy—and that they had been hoping for someone to end it.

One older woman approaches him, her eyes filled with fear and relief, and hands him a small, cloth-wrapped bundle. Inside is an old locket, which belonged to his family. "It's over now," she whispers, almost to herself, as though trying to convince herself as much as him.

As he leaves town, John Paul can't escape the feeling that the entity's influence hasn't entirely disappeared. Every mirror he passes catches his reflection with a flicker of something dark and unearthly, as though fragments of The Dweller are still embedded within him. The scars left by the mirror may have faded, but his soul feels marked, tethered to the horrors he faced within the mansion.

In the years that follow, John Paul remains haunted. He lives in isolation, avoiding mirrors and reflective surfaces, unable to shake the sense that his reflection isn't entirely his own. Though seemingly broken, The mirror's curse lingers subtly, and he becomes consumed by an unshakable paranoia that one day, The Dweller will find a way back.

John Paul is free yet bound by memories of darkness, glimpses of shadows that shouldn't exist, and the haunting feeling that some curses can never be completely broken. The terror he experienced continues to echo in his mind, a permanent reminder that the mansion's legacy, while buried, will never honestly be forgotten.

10

The Becoming

Elena Vanes, a driven but often-overlooked lab technician, is dedicated to studying atmospheric phenomena. One night, she notices an unusual weather pattern—a storm unlike anything recorded. Lightning flickers in shades of green, blue, and deep violet, sparking her scientific curiosity. Though her colleagues advise her to stay inside, she feels inexplicably drawn to the storm and steps outside for a closer look. As the wind howls, a bolt of lightning surges toward her, hitting her with brutal force. She blacks out, her mind filled with visions of ancient symbols and cryptic whispers. When she regains consciousness, she's alone in the dark, her body tingling with a strange energy.

At work, Elena feels something deeply unsettling; she's ravenous in a way food cannot satisfy. The day passes in a haze as her physical senses begin to shift. She starts to overhear faint whispers, and no one else notices. She feels her vision sharpening and can see details at incredible distances. At night, her hunger returns, now accompanied by the lingering symbols she saw during the storm, flashing in her mind with each craving. Her body aches, her skin prickles with energy, and she's tormented by images of her coworkers and neighbors, drawn to their life force with an almost predatory instinct.

Determined to fight the disturbing urges, Elena confines herself to her apartment, locking herself away from the people she now sees as prey. She tries to focus on work, revisiting her research to understand the storm and the strange symbols haunting her mind. But her visions become more vivid as the hours pass, and the whispers grow louder, almost as if they're calling to her. Her emotions amplify; minor irritations trigger near-violent impulses. She realizes her body and mind are changing—her anger, fear, and desires are more intense and uncontrollable than ever. Despite her horror, part of her embraces the change, wondering if this is a gift rather than a curse.

After days of isolation, Elena's hunger becomes unbearable. Feeling her body deteriorating without whatever it truly craves, she succumbs to the urge to go outside. That night, she encounters a stranger on the street, and as she passes them, the hunger overpowers her. She feels an impulse she can't resist and attacks, draining their life force. In a flash of clarity, she experiences an intoxicating surge of energy; her senses sharpen, her body strengthens, and her perception of reality intensifies. Looking at her reflection in a store window, she sees her eyes gleaming with a strange light, her face subtly shifting to a more predatory expression. Though horrified by what she's done, she feels a dark satisfaction. For the first time, she understands what she needs.

Now realizing the true nature of her powers, Elena tries to control them, exploring the limits of her abilities in private. Her physical skills are enhanced by each life force she takes, and she begins to heal almost instantly from injuries. The voices and symbols she glimpsed in her vision become clearer, warning her that she is no longer entirely human. She sees herself transforming in small ways—her teeth appear sharper, her fingers more claw-like, and her skin adopts a ghostly pallor. Desperate to find answers, she combs through ancient texts and online occult forums, discovering a name: "The Harbinger." She learns that the Harbinger is an entity that consumes fear and life to grow stronger, a being of darkness and destruction. Though she tries to resist, the pull of her monstrous side becomes more challenging to deny.

As Elena becomes bolder in her hunt, strange disappearances rattle the community. People report feeling an ominous presence around town, and a local news station picks up on a rash of unsolved cases, spreading fear throughout the area. Elena realizes that the ambient fear of the townspeople fuels her power even further; she can feel their terror like an electric current. She creeps through the streets at night, creating whispers of a "shadowy figure" that instills dread. Each fearful look and terrified whisper feeds her, and the power is intoxicating. She can feel herself changing, her mind darkening as her human empathy fades.

Desperate for clarity, Elena returns to the lab, hoping to uncover what triggered her transformation. Searching through records, she finds notes about a failed experiment involving atmospheric manipulation and ancient rituals. The project leader documented suspicions that they had unleashed something supernatural—something waiting for a host. She reads about a mythical entity called The Harbinger, who is said to bond with a human to become a creature of endless hunger and destruction. Suddenly, her coworker stumbles upon her in the lab, and the shock causes her monstrous instincts to take over. Driven by fear and hunger, she attacks, draining him of life, fully realizing her new identity. Elena has become The Harbinger, and her humanity now seems distant.

Fully embracing her transformation, Elena unleashes her powers, using her newfound strength and abilities to wreak havoc on the city. She no longer conceals herself; instead, she revels in terrorizing people, watching them scatter at the sight of her shadow. She feeds off their fear, using her abilities to create illusions and project dark energy, each new act of terror empowering her. Her appearance has shifted entirely—her eyes gleam like polished obsidian, her skin ashen, her form cloaked in shadows that swirl around her like a living mist. The townspeople give her a name: "The Harbinger," she finds herself reveling in the fear she commands. She is now a creature of chaos, and the city becomes her playground of terror.

After weeks of chaos, resistance forms among the town's researchers, led by a small group of scientists who studied with Elena. They recognize the patterns and connect her transformation to the ritual that unleashed The Harbinger. Armed with ancient relics and protective wards, they craft a trap to weaken and potentially banish her. When Elena enters the trap, she realizes too late that her power is being drained. For the first time, she feels pain, a searing weakness, as the group attempts to sever her connection to the dark powers. Though the battle leaves her severely weakened, she manages to escape, retreating to safety as her powers wane. The encounter shakes her confidence, forcing her to question her invincibility.

Wounded and desperate, Elena returns to the origin of her transformation—the site of the storm. She recalls the ritual text she read, realizing she must pass her curse to another host to survive. Summoning the last of her power, she performs a dark incantation, calling down another storm. Lightning strikes her, and her body dissipates into mist, merging with the storm as her essence fades. As the clouds clear, a new storm surrounds the city, and a young woman feels a strange pull. The Harbinger's legacy continues, waiting to emerge again in a new form.

11

The Legacy

Lena Grey, a quiet young artist haunted by dreams she can't understand, begins experiencing strange visions and sensations following a violent storm. She notices changes in herself: her senses are heightened, and her emotions are intense, almost overwhelming. Symbols flash through her mind—foreign and ancient—and an eerie voice whispers in her dreams, calling her "The Harbinger." Initially, she dismisses these as nightmares but soon realizes they aren't going away. She begins to sense a dark energy lurking within her, though she can't explain it.

As Lena's new abilities grow more robust, she loses control over her actions and emotions. She becomes prone to sudden, violent outbursts and feels an unsettling urge to dominate those around her. Her reflections seem to change subtly; her eyes are darker, and her shadow is longer. Terrified, she isolates herself, hoping to protect the people around her, especially her best friend, Claire, who has noticed her change. But each day, her powers intensify, and she starts hearing whispers calling her to act. She learns of recent reports about strange disappearances and rumors of "The Harbinger." Lena realizes this entity is tied to her—and that her powers and nightmares are connected to the horror spreading through the city.

Determined to understand what's happening to her, Lena delves into research, tracing rumors about the previous Harbinger's origins. She discovers stories of a woman named Elena Vanes, who disappeared after terrorizing the city. Lena realizes that Elena's powers are passed to her and that the Harbinger is a curse she has unknowingly inherited. Desperate for answers, she contacts survivors of Elena's attacks, who share terrifying accounts of their experiences. Lena fears that she's destined to become like Elena and begins searching for ways to break the curse before it consumes her entirely.

One night, desperate and sleep-deprived, Lena tries to draw out The Harbinger within her, testing if she can confront it directly. She sets up mirrors and dark candles, attempting an ancient ritual she found in Elena's research, hoping to communicate with the entity within. Suddenly, her reflection twists and changes; the face looking back at her is not her own but that of a monstrous version of herself with dark eyes and a malicious grin. The Harbinger speaks to her, telling her that resistance is futile—they are now one. Lena struggles against the dark force but feels it grows stronger daily.

In the days following her encounter with the Harbinger, Lena's powers grow exponentially, amplifying her fear and frustration. She develops the ability to manipulate shadows and create illusions that terrify others. When Claire notices Lena's change and confronts her, Lena loses control and unintentionally lashes out, causing Claire to collapse in terror. Horrified, Lena withdraws completely but realizes that the fear she inspires only strengthens the entity within her. Every frightening glance and rumor of a new Harbinger adds to her power. Lena struggles to retain control, but the Harbinger's hold tightens daily.

Overwhelmed by guilt and despair, Lena considers giving in to the Harbinger, convinced there's no escape from the curse. Her physical form continues to change, becoming shadow-like and spectral, with unnatural strength and agility. The Harbinger's voice taunts her, reminding her that only by embracing the darkness can she fulfill her potential. Lena finds herself torn between accepting her fate as The Harbinger or finding a way to escape it. Some of her is tempted by the power and influence she can wield, but her human side clings to the hope of freedom.

Determined to resist, Lena digs further into the curse's origins and learns of a ritual that could sever her bond with the Harbinger. She seeks out Father Simon, a priest who once performed exorcisms and is rumored to know about the supernatural. Father Simon is skeptical and fearful, but Lena's desperation convinces him to help her. He warns her that the Harbinger's hold will become permanent if she fails to complete the ritual. Lena agrees, knowing this is her last chance to reclaim her humanity, though the Harbinger mocks her efforts, whispering that no ritual can sever a bond that is "forever."

With Father Simon's guidance, Lena gathers the materials for the ritual, but she senses the Harbinger fighting back, its whispers now filled with fury and malice. As they perform the ritual, she experiences excruciating pain, and the entity within her begins to emerge, battling to maintain control. The ritual pushes the Harbinger out briefly, showing Lena a vision of Elena Vanes trapped in a nightmarish realm, a warning of what could happen if she fails. Just as the ritual nears completion, Lena feels a surge of darkness and collapses, the Harbinger reasserting its hold, leaving her weaker than before.

Disheartened by her failed attempt, Lena contemplates surrendering to the Harbinger's influence. Her appearance is nearly unrecognizable; her once-bright eyes are now deep black, and her skin is ashen. Father Simon, seeing the transformation, doubts she can be saved and informs the authorities, warning them of a "demon-possessed" woman. Betrayed, Lena barely escapes an ambush by the police, her powers triggered by the fear around her. She realizes she's losing herself to the Harbinger and that no one can be trusted, not even those who tried to help her.

With nowhere left to turn, Lena faces the Harbinger within her in a final confrontation. She returns to the site where the storm first struck, hoping the place of her transformation holds the key to ending the cycle. She enters a trance, forcing herself to confront the entity one last time. In the realm of shadows, she encounters Elena's spirit, who reveals that the Harbinger can be trapped but never destroyed. Lena must sacrifice her humanity and continue the curse or imprison herself in a dark limbo, forever restraining the Harbinger within.

In a heartbreaking choice, Lena decides to contain the Harbinger, sealing herself in the storm's origin to prevent it from passing to another host. As she fades into the shadows, she hears the Harbinger's final threat: "You can't imprison darkness... it will always return."

12

The Eternal Shadow

Alex Reeves, a seasoned journalist with a reputation for digging into the unusual, stumbles upon an old story about The Harbinger after a series of strange disappearances catches their attention. People are missing without a trace, and rumors of "a shadow that feeds on fear" circulate through the town. As Alex digs into the history of past Harbingers, from Elena Vanes to Lena Grey, they find threads of horror stretching back decades. Intrigued and skeptical, Alex decides to investigate further, unaware of how close they are to awakening the curse once more.

Alex's research takes them to old archives, where they discover photographs of Lena and sketches of Elena's monstrous transformation. They encounter an older man named Tommy Greer, a survivor of one of the Harbinger's attacks, who reveals haunting details about its power. Tommy warns Alex to stop digging, claiming anyone who investigates the Harbinger eventually falls prey to it. But Alex is undeterred, convinced that the Harbinger is nothing more than an urban legend. Yet, as they leave Tommy's house, Alex feels a chill, and a flickering shadow seems to follow them.

As Alex continues their investigation, strange occurrences begin to haunt them. They experience vivid nightmares of shadowy figures and wake up with bruises and cuts they can't explain. Shadows seem to cling to them, bending unnaturally, and Alex begins to sense something watching them. Their fear grows, feeding a dark presence they can't yet identify. Desperate for answers, Alex revisits Lena Grey's last known location—the storm site—where they feel an overpowering dread. Something stirs there, and Alex realizes they may be closer to the Harbinger than they thought.

One night, Alex wakes to find a mark on their arm: a series of symbols similar to those seen by Lena and Elena. Panicked, Alex reaches out to a local historian who has studied the occult aspects of the Harbinger. The historian explains that the mark is a form of "tagging," a sign that Alex has caught the Harbinger's attention. If they continue, the historian warns, the Harbinger might attempt to bond with them next. Terrified but curious, Alex debates abandoning the story, but their obsession with understanding the Harbinger's curse is too firm, and they continue their investigation.

Strange things begin happening to Alex. Their emotions become volatile, and they experience bursts of strength and a disturbing ability to manipulate shadows, though they can't fully control them. They start seeing visions of past Harbingers—Lena and Elena appear in their dreams, warning them to stop. Alex feels drawn to the storm site, sensing a powerful connection there. Each visit makes them feel the Harbinger's pull more acutely, but Alex convinces them they can resist it. Yet, their humanity seems to slip a little more each day, and their reflection changes.

One evening, while investigating a lead, Alex loses control and lashes out at someone who questions them. In a flash, they see their hands cloaked in shadows, the figure before them frozen in fear. Alex realizes that they've started feeding off others' terror. Horrified by their actions, Alex isolates themselves, trying to resist the urges that grow stronger by the hour. They feel the Harbinger within, an ever-present darkness pressing against their mind. The voice inside them whispers promises of power, taunting them to give in entirely.

Alex discovers they are not entirely lost yet—the bond with the Harbinger can be broken, but they'll need to act quickly. The historian they consulted earlier offers a potential solution: a dangerous ritual to exorcise the Harbinger before it takes complete control. However, the ritual requires Alex to confront the Harbinger directly in a liminal space, risking their life. Alex agrees, preparing mentally for a battle they know they may not survive. As the day of the ritual approaches, they begin to feel the Harbinger's strength weakening as fear gives way to a glimmer of hope.

During the ritual, Alex enters a trance and is transported to a shadowy realm where they come face-to-face with the Harbinger—a twisted version of themselves cloaked in darkness. The Harbinger reveals its origins, explaining that it's an ancient being, a force of terror that feeds off the human psyche. It has waited millennia, passing from host to host, growing stronger with each new body. The Harbinger offers Alex a choice: to surrender fully and embrace its power or to fight against it and risk being trapped in the shadow realm forever. Alex, torn between curiosity and fear, chooses to fight.

Alex struggles to overcome the Harbinger in the ensuing battle, but the entity is relentless, drawing upon centuries of strength. Each memory Alex has of loved ones, moments of courage, and instances of self-control weaken the Harbinger momentarily, but not enough to destroy it. Realizing that they can't defeat the Harbinger alone, Alex calls upon the memories of Lena and Elena, feeling the presence of their spirits fighting alongside them. Together, they force the Harbinger back, severing its bond with Alex's mind. But as Alex begins to awaken, they feel a residual darkness, knowing the Harbinger may still lurk within them.

Now free from the Harbinger's control, Alex returns to the real world, feeling changed yet victorious. They realize the Harbinger's curse may be weakened but not destroyed. Some of its powers linger, leaving Alex with a connection to shadows that's both unsettling and fascinating. Vowing to prevent the Harbinger from resurfacing, Alex becomes a guardian, using their residual powers to keep the entity contained and investigate supernatural threats. However, they know that the Harbinger is only dormant, waiting for the right moment to resurface in a new form. As Alex walks away from the storm site, they notice a faint flicker in their shadow—a reminder that some evils are never fully vanquished, only hidden.

13

The Final Shadow

Years have passed since Alex first confronted the Harbinger. Now a seasoned paranormal investigator, Alex monitors supernatural phenomena across the city. The Harbinger's influence remains dormant within them, but they sense a strange shift—an increase in strange disappearances, a familiar darkness that seems to pulse beneath the city's surface. Alex fears that the Harbinger is regaining strength; this time, it might not stay hidden. Their nights are haunted by visions of the Harbinger, its voice whispering, "I'm still here."

The darkness begins to reassert itself in ways Alex can't ignore. They see shadows moving independently, ominous symbols appearing in unexpected places, and hear eerie whispers growing louder daily. Despite their efforts, the connection they thought severed feels more like a door left ajar. One evening, Alex loses control during an investigation, and the Harbinger momentarily emerges, wreaking havoc on those around them. Horrified by the destruction, Alex realizes they're losing control over the darkness inside. The Harbinger is back; this time, it intends total domination.

Determined to protect those around them, Alex seeks help from an ancient order of supernatural scholars known as the Sons of Aether, who are rumored to possess knowledge of powerful containment rituals. The Sons of Aether agree to help but warn that separating Alex from the Harbinger might kill them both. They reveal that the Harbinger's influence has woven too deeply into Alex's spirit, meaning the ritual would require extreme measures. Though terrified, Alex knows they must try, significantly as the Harbinger's presence strengthens, threatening to consume them entirely.

The Sons of Aether prepare Alex for a ritual that will take them deep into their mind, into the heart of the shadow realm where the Harbinger resides. They warn Alex that, once there, they'll face not only the Harbinger but also their deepest fears. During the ritual, Alex slips into a trance, and their consciousness descends into a dark, twisted landscape, a realm of shadows where the Harbinger's power reigns supreme. Here, Alex is confronted by the spirits of past Harbingers—Lena, Elena, and others—all of whom warn them of the terrible price of failure.

Alex confronts a warped, monstrous version of themselves in the shadow realm, a manifestation of the Harbinger's darkness within. The creature taunts Alex, reminding them of the destruction they caused and the power they could wield if they stopped resisting. Alex fights back, but each attack only seems to strengthen the Harbinger. As they battle, Alex realizes they must confront their fears and regrets to weaken the Harbinger. In facing painful memories and moments of vulnerability, Alex chips away at the darkness, slowly reclaiming parts of themselves the Harbinger had taken.

After hours of battling the Harbinger, Alex is weakened, teetering on the edge of collapse. They realize that to break free fully, they must sacrifice the part of themselves tied to the Harbinger. Summoning the last of their strength, they tear away from their shadow, severing the connection in a burst of agony. The Harbinger recoils, weakened but not destroyed. Alex knows this severing will be temporary if they don't finish it in the real world. The Sons of Aether pull Alex back from the trance, warning them they're running out of time. Alex decides to attempt the only remaining way to end the Harbinger once and for all.

The Sons of Aether reveal a forbidden, dangerous spell that could banish the Harbinger permanently. Still, at a terrible cost, it will take the Harbinger and its current host into a permanent prison. Alex will need to sacrifice themselves to seal the entity away. Faced with the weight of the decision, Alex reaches out to loved ones and makes peace with their fate. Though afraid, they know they are the only ones who can contain the Harbinger. Preparing for the final confrontation, they go to the storm site where the curse first awakened within them.

Alex performs the spell at the storm site under the guidance of the Sons of Aether, calling upon every ounce of their strength. The Harbinger emerges in full force as the ritual unfolds, sensing its impending imprisonment. A brutal battle ensues between Alex and the Harbinger, who shifts between forms—shadow, monstrous specter, and human likenesses of past hosts, all taunting Alex. In a final act of courage, Alex opens their spirit, embracing the darkness fully so they can trap it within themselves. In that moment, they become a prison, absorbing the Harbinger completely.

The ritual completes as Alex's physical form vanishes, leaving only shadows and whispers of ancient words behind. The Sons of Aether perform a final seal on the storm site, binding it with charms and symbols to prevent the Harbinger's return. The city is quiet, the air still, as if the darkness has been lifted. Those who knew Alex mourn their loss but remember them as heroes, guardians who gave their lives to keep others safe. Though the Harbinger is gone, the Sons of Aether remain vigilant, knowing darkness often finds a way back.

Years pass, and the storm site becomes a place of superstition, a reminder of the strange and terrifying events that once plagued the city. Few remember Alex's name, but a new generation of Sons of Aether monitors the site, watching for any signs of the Harbinger's return. The city remains safe, untouched by past horrors, yet some say they hear whispers on stormy nights, faint shadows moving where none should. The Harbinger's legend lives on, a reminder that though evil can be contained, it can never be truly erased.

Though Alex sacrificed themselves to contain the Harbinger, traces of their spirit linger. Those who visit the storm site and listen carefully on quiet nights say they can hear a voice urging them to stay vigilant and warn of shadows yet unseen. Some wonder if Alex's spirit guards the place, standing watch against future threats. Others believe it's simply the wind, but Alex's story endures in the hearts of those who remember—a tale of courage, darkness, and sacrifice that inspires them to keep the shadows at bay.

Their legacy lives on, serving as both a warning and a beacon of hope to those who might one day confront similar darkness. The series concludes with the understanding that while true evil may never disappear, the bravery of individuals can hold it back, one sacrifice at a time.